Taking Flight

A story about embracing who you are!

Mrs. Beaver was the best flight teacher in the entire world. Mrs. Beaver loved her class of eager learners.

Every day after Lunch, Mrs. Beaver would lock her door, put the class key around her neck and the class would go learn to fly. She would teach her group of new flyers how to fly high and fast.

Mrs. Beaver had a very talented class. Some of the fastest flyers she had ever seen!

There was Tommy the Golden Eagle, Maggie the Falcon, Jessie the Needletail, Bobby the Humming-bird—Bobby could even fly backwards and forward! Last but not least, there was Frankie the Penguin.

Frankie was just like all the little birdies of the class. Frankie was a smart student. He knew his ABC's, all his colors and he even knew how to count all the way to 1000.

Frankie had one thing that was different about him. Frankie was a penguin and penguins can't fly. No matter how hard Frankie tried, he could not fly.

Sometimes Frankie would feel sad because his friends would make fun of him for not being able to fly. Frankie did not want to be different. He wanted to be like everyone else.

Every day, when the class was out flying, Frankie had to wait by the pond.

One day the class was flying, and Mrs. Beaver was teaching a new trick. As she was teaching, the class key around her neck fell into the deep pond.

The water was deep, cold and dark. None of the students could dive that deep, not even the teacher!

"I can do it!" said a small voice.
It was Frankie.

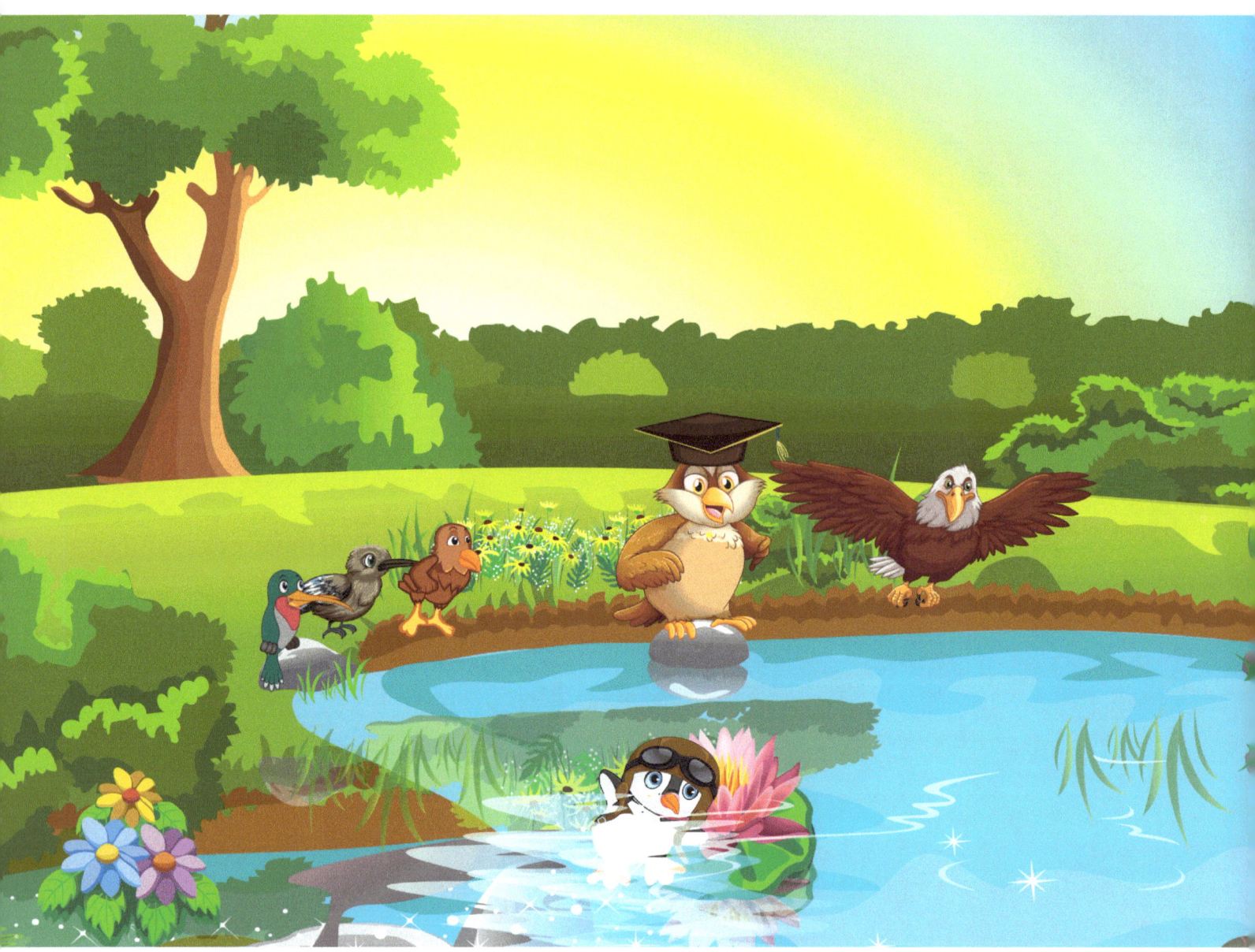

Frankie jumped into the water and went all the way down to the bottom. Everyone was scared, but not Frankie. Two minutes later Frankie jumped out of the water holding the key in his mouth. Everyone cheered.

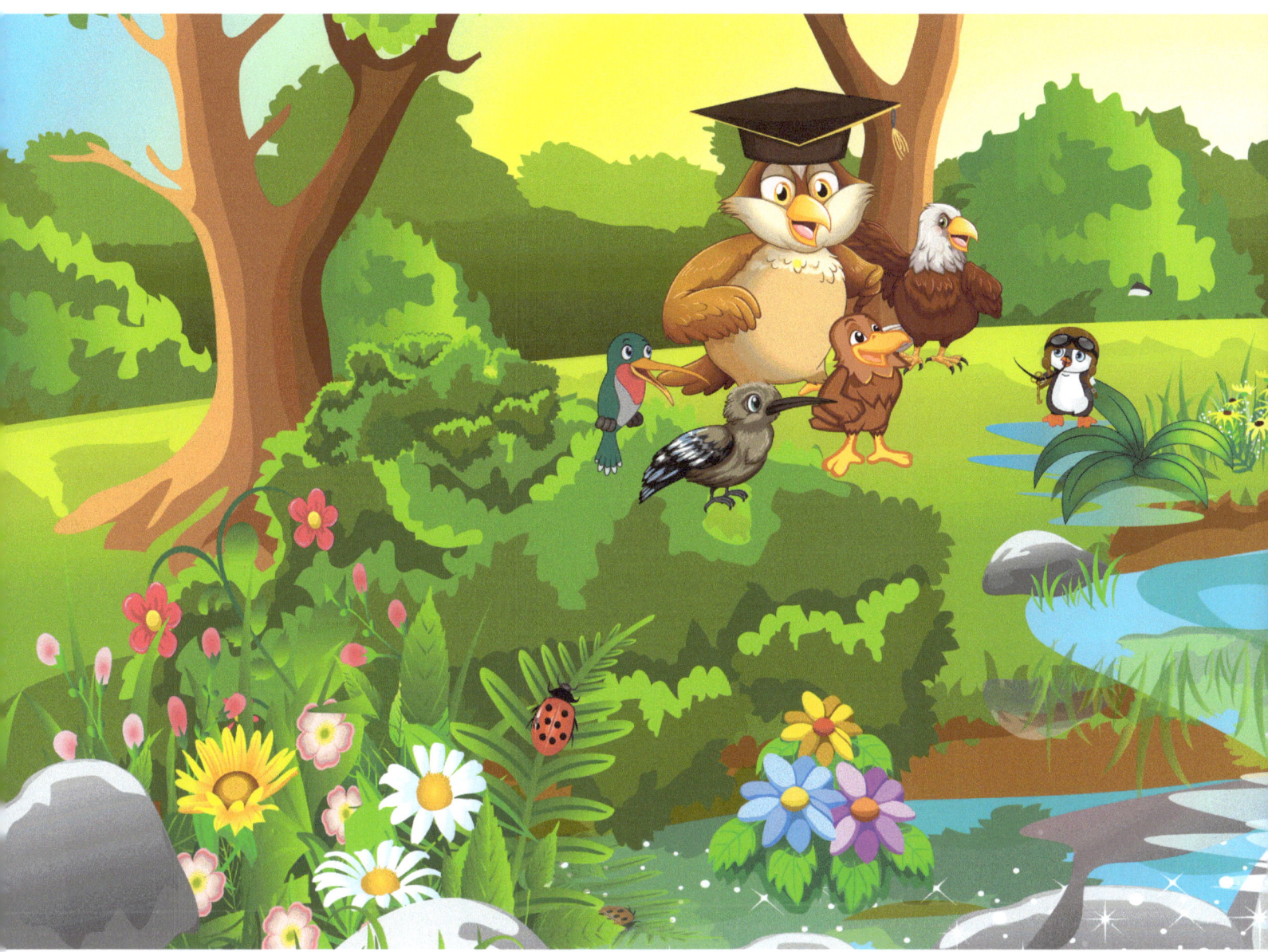

"Thank you, Frankie!" exclaimed Mrs. Beaver. "You saved the day!"

"Everyone gather around!" said Mrs. Beaver. "Class we are all different for a reason. Frankie may not be able to fly high and fast, but he can swim fast and deep. It is because Frankie is different he was able to rescue the class key. Being different is a good thing because it means we all have something to offer."

All the students gave Frankie a hug,
and Mrs. Beaver shouted, "Class! Say it with me:
We are all different for a reason!"

From that day forward, no one made fun of Frankie. Everyone loved Frankie because he was different.

Be

YOU

Are!

To my nephews and niece
I love you all!